The
NORTH
WIND
and the
SUN
and Other Fables of Aesop

The
NORTH
WIND
and the
SUN
and Other Fables of Aesop

Translated by Gregory McNamee

DAIMON
VERLAG

These translations are based on original Greek texts collected by Ben Edwin Perry in *Aesopica* (Urbana: University of Illinois Press, 1952) and other sources.

ISBN 3-85630-636-6

Book cover and contents designed by Kim Long.
Cover art adapted from a Richard Heighway illustration from
The Fables of Aesop (Joseph Jacobs, Shocken Books, 1894).
The illustrations in the contents are mostly from a variety of
books on Aesop's fables published in the mid- to late-1800s,
reprinted courtesty of the Juvenile Historical Collection of
the Denver Public Library, Denver, Colorado.

Printed in Canada

for Brianna

Introduction

For more than two thousand years, children throughout the world have been hearing the fables of Aesop.

The stories have traveled far from their homeland in Asia Minor, and as they have traveled, they have changed to reflect the people who told them. Here is one of them, as Aesop told it:

> *One day a hare ridiculed the short feet and slow movements of a tortoise, who replied, "You may think that you're as swift as the wind, but I promise you, I'll win in a race against you."*
>
> *The hare accepted the tortoise's bet. The two started off together. The tortoise kept on plodding along, not once stopping, keeping a slow and steady pace to the end of the course. The hare, lying down on a soft patch of grass to catch its breath, fell fast asleep. When he awoke, he saw the tortoise crossing the finish line far ahead.*

Contests, Aesop seems to be telling us, are not always won by the fastest—or the strongest, or the most beautiful. In Aesop's world, the meek and powerless have their day, too. A Native American storyteller made the same point with a version of the fable told in the 1890s.

> *Rabbit was a great runner, and everybody knew it. No one thought Turtle anything but a slow traveler, but he was a great warrior and very boastful, and the two were always disputing about their speed. At last they agreed to decide the matter by a race. They*

7

fixed the day and the starting place and arranged to run across four mountain ridges, and the one who came in first at the end was to be the winner.

The Rabbit felt so sure of it that he said to Turtle, "You know you can't run. You can never win the race, so I'll give you the first ridge and then you'll have only three to cross while I go over four."

Turtle said that would be all right, but that night when he went home to his family he sent for his turtle friends and told them he wanted their help. He said he knew he could not outrun Rabbit, but he wanted to stop Rabbit's boasting. He explained his plan to his friends and they agreed to help him.

When the day came all the animals were there to see the race. Rabbit was with them, but Turtle had gone ahead toward the first ridge, as they had arranged, and they could hardly see him on account of the long grass. Then Rabbit started off with long jumps up the mountain, expecting to win the race before Turtle could get down the other side. But before he got up the mountain he saw Turtle go over the ridge ahead of him. He ran on, and when he reached the top he looked all around, but could not see Turtle on account of the long grass. He kept on down the mountain and began to climb the second ridge, but when he looked up again there was Turtle just going over the top. Now he was surprised and made his longest jumps to catch up, but when he got to the top there was Turtle away in front going over the third ridge. Rabbit was getting tired now and nearly out of breath, but he kept on down the mountain and

up the other ridge until he got to the top just in time
to see Turtle cross the fourth ridge and win the race.

Turtle, you see, cheated. Because, at least in Rabbit's eyes, all turtles look alike, Turtle simply posted his friends along the racecourse and made sure that one turtle or another was always ahead of the competition. Even with this twist, though, we can see the similarities between this Cherokee story and the ancient Greek original.

We have hundreds of stories attributed to Aesop, and thousands more variants of those stories told by cultures around the world. Yet about Aesop we know almost nothing—not even whether he existed.

The storyteller we call Aesop is said to have been a Greek slave who lived from about 620 to 564 b.c. Legend says that his owner, Iadmon of Samos, freed Aesop after hearing his pointed tales; Aesop used the occasion of his freedom to travel throughout Asia Minor and Greece, collecting still more folk stories and telling them to audiences. In his Rhetoric, Aristotle credits Aesop for having defended a corrupt politician by telling this fable:

> *A hedgehog, taking pity on a flea-infested fox,*
> *asked whether he could remove the vermin with his*
> *quills. The fox replied, "No, these fleas are full of*
> *blood, so they no longer bother me. If you take them*
> *off, fresh fleas will come."*

Just so, Aesop said to the jury, if this man is removed from office, a new one will come along and rob the city all over again. Herodotus tells us that Aesop was murdered by the citizens of Delphi, perhaps because stories like this one struck uncomfortably close to home.

We know little more about Aesop, and the stories assigned to him as the Fables are doubtless the work of many hands over generations, as with the Homeric epics. Still, those stories are ours to enjoy, to learn from, to teach from; like all folktales, they offer, as the French anthropologist Claude Lévi-Strauss observed, tools that are good to think with. Stories that enrich the imagination and subtly impart moral lessons of great value, these fables are now part of the intellectual inheritance of the species, and we can only hope that our children, and their children's children, will tell them years from now, just as people have been telling them across the centuries, allowing them to endure for thousands of years to come, ever changing, ever growing.

The North Wind and the Sun

A lion caught a rabbit and was about to eat it when a deer came running by. The lion took off after the deer, and the rabbit escaped. The lion could not catch the deer and came back to eat the rabbit, but found that it was gone.

"I deserve this," he said. "I let go of what I had in hope of finding something better."

One day the rabbits gathered to talk about the frightening world they lived in, where people, dogs, eagles, and hawks chased after them. They agreed that a life filled with such things was not worth living, and they ran to a pond to drown themselves.

When the frogs who lived in the pond heard the rabbits' long legs pounding on the ground, they jumped into the water. One of the rabbits said to the others, "Stop! Things aren't so bad after all. Look: some creatures are even more afraid than we are!"

A vixen sneered at a lioness because she could bear only one child at a time.

"Yes, that's right," the lioness said. "But that one child is a lion."

The mice were once at war with the weasels. Whenever they fought against the weasels, who were bigger and stronger than they were, the mice always lost.

The mice decided that they needed stronger leaders, and they chose as generals the strongest of their kind. To make it known that they were more important than the other mice, the generals made helmets out of deer antlers.

The mice went out to fight the weasels. As always, the weasels drove them back to their burrows. They all slipped quickly into their holes except the generals, whose helmets got tangled up in the dirt and grass. The weasels caught the generals and ate them.

A country mouse invited his city cousin to come to dinner. The city mouse was disappointed to see that the meal consisted only of wheat and barley. He said, "How poorly you live! Come home with me and I'll give you a feast."

The two went off to the city, and came to a house full of peas, beans, bread, fruits, cheese, and honey. Seeing all these good things, the country mouse agreed that his kitchen was poor indeed.

They were about to eat when the door opened and a man came in, so they ran into a hole and hid. The man left and they came back out to return to their meal. But then a woman came in, and they hid again.

The country mouse said goodbye. "All this good food isn't worth all this fear and danger," he said. "I prefer wheat and barley to constant alarm."

So many people stepped on a certain snake that it went crawling up Mount Olympus to ask Zeus for help.

Zeus said, "If you had bitten the first person who stepped on you, the rest would take more care about where they walked."

A man and a lion were traveling together through forested mountains. To pass the time, they began to boast to each other of their strength and agility. They argued back and forth for many miles, until they came to an abandoned temple with a stone statue before it depicting an athlete strangling a lion.

The man pointed it out and said, "You see! We humans are the strongest creatures on earth."

The lion answered, "A human made this statue. If lions could sculpt, it would tell an entirely different story."

A wolf happened to pass by the door of a hut in which some shepherds sat gorging themselves on a roasted leg of lamb. The wolf said to them, "Think how you'd behave if I did what you're doing!"

The animals of the forest gathered at a splendid feast one night. As they ate, a monkey stood up and danced for them, ending his performance to tremendous applause.

A camel, envious of the monkey's success, stood up in turn and began to dance. He moved so clumsily that the rest of the animals booed him out of their assembly.

Once a wolf decided to disguise himself so that he could forage for food without alarming anyone. He wrapped himself in a sheepskin and browsed with a pasturing flock. The shepherd was none the wiser, and when evening came, he closed the wolf up with the rest of the sheep in their fold, locking the gate behind him.

The wolf was about to spring upon a lamb when the shepherd returned, looking for his supper. Still tricked by the disguise, the shepherd caught the wolf and killed him with his knife.

The north wind and the sun argued over who was the strongest, and they decided to have a contest over who could make a traveler passing by take off his coat.

The north wind went first. It blew hard, but the traveler wrapped his coat around him even tighter to keep out the blast.

The wind blew harder, and the man stopped and pulled a blanket from his knapsack and wrapped it around himself. The wind finally grew tired.

Then the sun shone down warmly, so that the traveler removed the blanket. The sun blazed, and the traveler took off his coat and went swimming in a nearby stream.

An astronomer used to wander outside each night to observe the heavens. One evening, as he wandered through town with his eyes fixed on the sky, he fell into a deep well. He cried for help until a neighbor arrived and called down to him.

Learning what had happened, the neighbor said, "Why pry into the heavens when you cannot see what is here on the earth?"

A bee from Mount Hymettos flew up to the summit of Mount Olympus to give Zeus some fresh honey from her hive. Zeus, delighted by her gift, offered her whatever she wished in return.

She said, "My lord, please give me the ability to sting, so that I can punish any human who tries to steal my honey."

Zeus, who loved humans, was displeased, but he did not go back on his promise. He replied, "You will have your wish, but it will be at your own risk. By resorting to the use of your weapons, you too will die."

A wolf got the bone of a bird stuck in its throat. He persuaded a crane to put her head into his throat and remove the bone, promising her a great reward.

The crane extracted the offending bone and asked to be paid. The wolf grinned, baring his teeth, and said, "It seems to me you've been paid. After all, I let you draw your head from my jaws."

A mule, stumbling under a heavy load of wood, slipped off the path and splashed into a pond. He groaned heavily. Some frogs in the pond said to him, "Why make such a fuss over a little water? We have to live here all the time."

A thirsty crow saw a pitcher and went to get a drink of water from it. He soon saw, however, that the water was so low that he could not get at it. He collected as many stones as he could carry and dropped them with his beak one by one into the pitcher, until the water rose to meet his beak.

An eagle and a fox decided to build their homes next door to each other. The eagle built a nest in a tall tree, while the fox crept into the bushes and there bore her young. While the fox was off hunting, the eagle swooped down and carried off her kits so that her eaglets would have something to eat.

The fox returned. She was angry at the eagle — but mostly because she could think of no way to avenge herself.

The eagle then swooped down on a nearby altar and stole a piece of a goat that was being sacrificed. A spark remained on the goat's singed skin, and it set the eagle's nest afire. The eaglets were burned and fell to the bottom of the tree, where the fox ate them in full sight of the eagle.

A wolf, happening on a lost lamb, decided not to eat it straightaway without first proving that he had a right to do so. "Last year you insulted me," the wolf said. "No, sir," the lamb replied. "I wasn't even born last year." "Well, then," the wolf said, "you've been feeding in my pasture." "No, sir," the lamb said. "I haven't yet tasted grass." "You've been drinking out of my well," the wolf said. "No, sir," the lamb answered. "I am still drinking my mother's milk." "Well," said the wolf — for a tyrant is always a tyrant — "for all that, I'm not going to go without my supper."

A man who was bitten by a dog went to see about a cure for his fever. The doctor said, "If you want to be cured, take a piece of bread, dip it into your blood, and give it to the dog who bit you." The man laughed and said, "If I did that, I would be inviting every dog in town to bite me."

A peacock once complained to Hera that, while the nightingale pleased every ear with its beautiful song, he could barely get a sound out without the whole world laughing at him.

Hera replied, "But you are so handsome. An emerald shines in your collar, and a palette of color glows in your tail."

"What use is beauty without a song to proclaim it?" asked the peacock.

"The Fates have distributed qualities all around," Hera said. "To you went beauty. The eagle was given strength. The nightingale got its lovely song. The raven brings good luck, the crow bad. Imagine what would happen if they, too, wanted to have it all."

An amaranth, planted in a garden next to a rose bush, said to it, "What a beautiful flower you are, loved by mortals and the gods alike. I envy your appearance and your sweet fragrance."

The rose bush replied, "I should envy you. I live for a season, while you live forever, blooming each year in endless youth. No careless hand comes along to pick you and kill you. Take my word for it: you have nothing to envy me for."

A farmer found an eagle caught in a trap. He admired the eagle's beauty so much that he let it go. The eagle flew off.

Seeing the farmer sitting one day underneath an old wall, the eagle swooped down and stole his hat. The farmer jumped up and chased the eagle, and the eagle dropped the hat. When he came back he saw that the wall had toppled over. The eagle had just saved his life.

A raven sat on the branch of a fig tree waiting for the fruit to ripen. Day after day he sat there.

A fox passing by said to him, "Too much hope will only disappoint you—and it surely won't feed you."

A weasel found a bat that had fallen to the ground. The bat begged the weasel to spare his life. The weasel refused, saying that by nature he was an enemy of all birds. The bat said, "I'm not a bird, but a mouse." The weasel let him go.

Not long afterward, the bat met another weasel. The weasel said, "The mice are my sworn enemies." The resilient bat said, "It's a good thing that I'm a bird!"

A mule, hearing some grasshoppers chirping, became enchanted by their song and decided to live as they did. He asked the grasshoppers what they ate that gave them such beautiful voices. "The dew," the grasshoppers replied. The mule resolved to live on dew from then on, and within a few days he was dead.

A boy was out hunting for locusts. As he caught them, he almost scooped up a scorpion. The scorpion showed his stinger and said, "If you had touched me, you would have lost me — and all your locusts, too!"

A rooster, scratching at the ground for food, turned up a gem. The rooster said, "I have no use for such things. I would rather have a single barleycorn than all the jewels in the world."

A pomegranate and an apple tree were once arguing loudly over who was the more beautiful. A bramble raised its head from a nearby hedge and said, "My friends, in my presence you should find something else to do besides carry on such vain disputes."

A farmer set out nets on a newly plowed field and caught several cranes that had come to pick at his seed. Among the cranes was a stork, who said, "Please let me go. I come from a fine family. I'm a stork, a fine and noble bird. Look at my feathers and you'll see for yourself."

The farmer replied, "All I know is that I caught you with these robbers, and with them you must die."

Some flies once swarmed to an overturned honeypot and settled into the honey to eat. Stuck fast, they began to suffocate. "How stupid we are," one of the flies said. "We have killed ourselves for the sake of a little pleasure."

A miser sold all that he owned and bought a lump of gold, which he buried in a hole in the ground. Every day he went to the site and studied the ground for any sign of disturbance. One of his workmen observed the miser's daily visits and decided to follow him. He discovered the miser's secret and dug up the gold. The next day the miser found the hole and began to weep loudly. A neighbor came to see what was wrong. When he learned of the miser's loss, he said, "Don't cry. Why don't you just take an ordinary stone, put it into the ground, and pretend that the gold is still there? It'll do you the same good — for when you had the gold you buried it away and did not put it to any use."

A piglet, a sheep, and a goat were standing in a field. A shepherd came along and grabbed the piglet, which squealed loudly and slipped out of the shepherd's grasp, crying loudly all the while. The sheep and the goat said, "Why do you have to make such a racket? The shepherd is always putting his hands on us." The piglet said, "When the shepherd touches you, it's for wool or milk. When he touches me, it's for my life."

A boy put his hand into a pitcher full of filberts. He grabbed as many as his hand could hold, but he found that he could not pull his hand out of the pitcher. He burst into tears. A passerby said, "Be satisfied with half as much, and you'll be free."

Some boys were out skipping stones across a pond. Many of the stones found targets in the frogs who lived there. One of the frogs raised its head from the water and said, "Boys, please stop. What is sport to you is death to us."

A lion, weary on a hot day, lay down for a nap. A mouse ran through his mane and into his ears, then scampered away. The lion rose and pawed at the ground, enraged, looking for the mouse. A fox happened by and said, "My, my. Why are you so afraid of a little mouse?" "It's not that I'm afraid," the lion said. "It's just that I resent his familiarity."

A middle-aged man courted two women, a
young one and an old one. The old woman,
ashamed of being seen with a man so young,
plucked out a few of his black hairs every time the
man came calling. The young woman, on the other
hand, plucked out his gray hairs, ashamed to be
seen with a man so old. In no time at all the man
was bald.

"Why should there be such fear and hatred among us?" the wolves said to the sheep. "It's all the dogs' fault. They attack us whenever we come near you, making us think that you are our enemies." The sheep dismissed the dogs and said, "Let there be peace among us." The wolves fell on the flock and destroyed it at leisure.

A vine grew heavy with grapes and leaves. A hungry goat came by and nibbled at it. The vine said, "Why do you injure me without cause? Can't you eat grass? But it doesn't matter. I'll have my revenge soon, for even if you cut me down to the roots and chop off all my leaves, I'll still have wine to offer when you are led to the altar in sacrifice."

A mouse, who always lived on the land, fell into company with a frog. The frog said, "Since we're such good friends, we should yoke ourselves together with this rope." The frog and the mouse went into a field and began to eat seeds. Then the frog dragged the mouse to his pond and jumped in. The frog croaked happily as if he had done something good. The mouse soon drowned, and his body bobbed on the surface of the pond. A hawk happened by and scooped the mouse's body up, and the frog went along to be eaten as well.

A horse and a donkey went traveling with their owner. The donkey said to the horse, "Please take part of my load and help me." The horse refused, and the donkey, broken by fatigue, died.

The owner put the donkey's load on the horse. The horse began to whinny in pain.

"If I had only helped" it cried, "I would have had a light load, and not all of this!"

A crow happened to steal a bit of meat. The crow sat in a tree proudly with the meat held fast in her beak. A fox who wandered by saw the meat and said to the crow, "How beautiful you are! If only your voice matched your beauty, you would be the queen of all birds!" The crow, anxious to show off her voice, began to caw loudly and dropped the meat. The fox ran off, turning to say, "My dear, your voice is really all right, but your intellect is another thing altogether."

A certain dog was in the habit of sneaking up on people and biting them, and so its owner hung a bell around its neck so that everyone heard him coming. The dog trotted down to the marketplace and tossed his head around to shake the bell.

Another dog said, "Why act so proud? That bell is not a reward, but a punishment. You tried to hide your nature, but you were found out."

The first ant started life as a human, a farmer who worked hard but who also stole his neighbors' crops. Zeus changed him into an insect, but his nature stayed the same. To this day he marches back and forth, taking his neighbors' crops.

A dog took up residence in a manger. It would not eat the barley in it, but neither would it let the horse who fed on it come anywhere close.

An ant worked hard all summer gathering bits of wheat and barley to store up for the winter. A beetle, passing by, laughed at the ant for working so hard when most other creatures took a holiday. The ant said nothing.

When winter arrived with its rain and snow, the beetle came to the ant and begged for food. "Instead of spending your time laughing at me you should have worked," the ant replied. "You would have plenty of food if you had."

The rivers got together to complain about the ocean. "When we come to you, you turn our fresh waters salty and undrinkable."

The ocean answered, "Well, don't come to me, then."

A horse had a wide plain all to himself. A stag came along and browsed on his pasture.

The horse, angry at having to share, asked a passing man if he would help him by killing the stag. "I will," said the man, "but only if you'll let me put this bit in your mouth."

The horse did, and the man climbed on his back. They drove the stag away, but from that day on the horse was a slave.

Zeus made the animals before he made humans, and he gave them powers like speed and strength. The humans then complained that they had been left out, with all the good things taken.

Zeus said, "I gave you the ability to think. That is the greatest thing you could have. It makes you stronger and faster than any other creature."

The humans realized what had been given to them, and they honored Zeus for his generosity.

An old farmer wanted his sons to become good farmers, too. He called them and said, "Boys, I won't be around much longer. I've hidden your inheritance out in the fields, and there you will find my final gift to you." Then he died.

The sons thought there was a vast treasure on their farm, and they turned up every bit of the soil. They found no treasure, but the soil was so well worked that they had a magnificent crop that year.

A hunter asked a forester if he had seen a lion's tracks nearby. The forester said that he would take him to see the lion itself. The hunter turned pale and said in fright, "I only asked you about the tracks — not the lion!"

A shepherd once brought his flock to the sea, where he admired its cool, calm waters. He decided to travel on the sea as a merchant, so he sold his flock and bought a load of dates. A terrible storm blew up, and it looked as if his ship would sink unless the shepherd abandoned his cargo. Later, in port, another trader pointed out how calm the sea was. "I think," the shepherd said, "that it's just hungry for some more dates."

A shepherd found a wolf cub and raised it. He taught it how to steal lambs from other shepherd's flocks.

The young wolf said to him, "You've taught me well—so well that you'd better keep an eye out on your own flocks from now on."

A donkey climbed up on the roof of a building and frisked about so energetically that it broke through the tiles. Its angry owner shouted at the donkey to get down. The donkey said, "Yesterday a monkey did the same thing, and you laughed and laughed!"

Once a lion woke up to find a mouse climbing on him. The lion caught the mouse and was about to kill it. The mouse cried out, "If you save my life, I'll be sure to return the favor."

The lion laughed at the thought of a mouse saving his life, but it let the mouse go free all the same. Not long after that, a hunter trapped the lion and tied it up with stout ropes. The mouse heard the lion roar and gnawed the ropes through with his sharp teeth, saying, "You laughed when I said I would save your life. Now you know that even a mouse can help a lion."

A dog who had a fondness for stealing eggs saw an oyster lying in a pail, and he ate it up in a gulp. He immediately got a stomachache and realized, as he later said, "It was silly of me to think that everything round is an egg."

A fox who tried to swim across a wide river was carried off by the current into a deep canyon. There it crawled to shore and lay down to rest and see to its wounds. Soon it was covered by lice. A hedgehog who came by asked whether the fox wanted help in removing the lice. "No, thank you," said the fox. "These are already on me, and they're full. If you get rid of them new ones will come along, and they'll be hungry."

Some dogs once found a lion skin and began to rip it to pieces with their teeth and claws. A fox passing by said, "If this lion were still alive, you wouldn't act so fierce."

The animals once had as their king a lion. He was not angry or cruel, but just and kind. During his reign he issued a royal decree saying that from then on the wolves and lambs, panthers and kids, tigers and deer, and dogs and rabbits would live in peace and friendship. A rabbit said, "I have longed to see this day, when the strong would let the weak alone." And at that the rabbit ran away.

A farmer and his wife had a hen that laid a
golden egg every day. They lived well but wanted
more still, and so they killed the hen, believing
that she had a big chunk of gold inside her. To
their surprise they found that the hen was just the
same as any other hen, and from that day on they
lamented having thrown away their comfortable
lives in the hope of becoming rich instantly.

A groom who was hired to take care of a champion horse did a good job of brushing its coat every day, but he also stole the horse's oats and sold them to other grooms. The horse said, "If you really cared about my well-being, you'd spend less time grooming me and more time feeding me."

A traveler once hired a donkey and its owner to take him across the desert. The day was very hot, and the men stopped to rest. They argued over who would sit in the donkey's shadow. The traveler said that he had hired the donkey, but the owner said that the fee did not include the shadow.

While the two men argued, the donkey ran away, taking its shadow with it.

A man came into the forest and asked the trees if he could cut one of them down to make a handle for a piece of metal that he had. The trees allowed him to cut down a young ash.

The man put the handle on the metal and made an ax. He started to cut down all the trees he could. An old oak said to a cedar next to it, "We should have said no and kept on living forever. Sacrificing one of us has cost us all our lives."

A kid was clambering about on the roof of a house. It looked down and saw a wolf passing by, and began to call the wolf names. The wolf said, "Just remember, you're not the one who's mocking me. It's the roof you're standing on."

A dog was crossing a bridge with a big piece of meat in its mouth. It looked down in the water and saw its reflection. Thinking that the reflection was another dog with a bigger piece of meat, it let the meat go and started snapping at the reflection. The river carried the meat away, and the dog went hungry.

A hungry fox saw some fine-looking black grapes hanging down from a vine. The fox jumped as high as it could, trying to reach the grapes. Hours later, it still could not reach them. Disappointed, the fox said, "Well, I'll bet they were sour anyway."

A philosopher, standing on the seashore, happened to witness a shipwreck in which the crew and the passengers all drowned. He cried out to the heavens, "There is no obviously no justice in the universe, seeing that all those innocent people just died!" He did not see that he was standing on an ant's nest. When one of the ants stung him, the philosopher immediately stamped on the whole colony, killing hundreds of ants with his foot. The god Hermes happened by, and he hit the philosopher over the head with his wand, saying, "Who are you to judge the ways of the gods, seeing what you've just done to those poor ants?"

A woodman, cutting trees by a riverbank, dropped his ax into a deep pool. Being unable now to earn his living, he sat on the bank and cried. Hermes happened by and asked what had happened. The woodman told Hermes of his troubles. Hermes plunged into the river and returned with a golden ax in his hand, asking the woodman whether this were the one he lost. "No," the woodman replied, "that's not mine." Hermes dove into the water again and returned with a silver ax. "That's not mine," the woodman said again. Finally Hermes returned with the woodman's ax. "Because you did not lie to me," Hermes said, "you may have your ax. And you may keep the others, too."

The woodman raced home and told his friends what had happened. One of them decided to try for himself. He ran to the river, tossed his ax into the stream, and began to weep. Hermes appeared, plunged into the stream, and brought up the golden ax. When the fellow said, "That's mine!" Hermes dropped it into the river and left, refusing even to retrieve the simple ax the man had thrown away.

A peacock spread out its beautiful tail for a crane who was passing by, making fun of the crane's pale feathers. "I have a robe like a king's," the peacock said, "in all the colors of the rainbow. You don't have any color in yours!"

"You're right," said the crane, "but I can fly to the highest heavens, while you're stuck here on earth."

A swallow and a crow were once arguing about whose plumage was prettier. The crow put an end to the argument by saying, "Your feathers are pretty in the springtime, but mine protect me against the winter."

A flea once landed on a wrestler's bare foot and bit it. The wrestler loudly cried out to Herakles, begging for help. The flea bit the wrestler's foot a second time, at which the wrestler said, "O Herakles! If you can't protect me from a flea, how are you going to save me from my opponents?"

A horse, an ox, and a dog asked a man to provide them with shelter from the cold. The man built a fire and welcomed the animals. He gave the horse plenty of oats, the ox plenty of hay, and the dog plenty of meat.

Grateful to him, the animals decided to give all humans some of their qualities in return. The horse gave humans the impetuousness, strength, and stubbornness of youth. The ox gave the fondness for work of middle age. But the dog, that tricky creature, gave the irritability and fear of strangers of old age.

Zeus once gathered the animals and said he would offer a prize for the one with the best-looking child. A monkey came up with a newborn, which of course had no hair, a flat nose, and wrinkled skin.

The other animals laughed, but the monkey said, "Whether Zeus gives me the prize or not, in my eyes this is the most beautiful child of all."

A farmer had an apple tree in his garden. It bore no fruit, but birds and grasshoppers lived happily in it. The farmer decided to cut it down and started to chop at its roots.

The birds and grasshoppers begged him not to cut down the tree, saying that if he let it live they would sing for him by day and night. The farmer ignored them and kept cutting. In the hollow he made he found a hive full of honey. He tasted a piece of honeycomb and dropped his ax at once, so delicious was the taste.

From that day on he took good care of the tree.

Some travelers, weary in the heat of the summer sun, lay under the spreading branches of a plane tree to rest. As they lay there, one of the travelers said, "You know, the plane tree is quite useless. It doesn't bear any fruit, and its wood doesn't burn well." The plane tree said, "Fine talk! How can you criticize me while resting in my shade?"

Every one of us carries two packs, one in front and one behind. The one in front is full of other people's faults, while the one behind is full of our own flaws. Because we cannot see our shortcomings, we imagine ourselves to be perfect—but we are all too quick to see the faults of others.

Once a certain lion, the king of the forest, decided that the other animals should surrender a part of their prey as tax. The lion had trouble figuring out how to impose this tax fairly, however.

The wise elephant said, "Tax people's virtues, and leave it to your subjects to list all the good qualities they have. Their vanity should turn a handsome profit."

Zeus called together all the animals one day to say that if they wanted to change any aspect of their appearance, they could ask him to do so.

The monkey said, "My looks are just fine, but you might ask the bear over there."

The bear growled, "There's nothing wrong with me, but you might make the elephant's ears a bit shorter and tail a bit longer."

The elephant trumpeted, "I'm fine, but the whale really needs to be smaller."

The ant said, "The gnat is too small."

And so it went, until Zeus became angry at their vanity and sent the animals away.

An owl who saw a mistletoe seed sprout urged the other birds to pull it up so that it could not grow up to make the poison that humans used to capture them. The owl also advised them to pull up flax seed, from which humans made nets to capture birds, and to gather up feathers so that humans could not use them on their arrows.

The birds ignored the owl and went about their business. But soon enough they found that the owl was right, and they declared that the owl was the wisest of birds.

But the owl no longer bothers to give them advice.

A mule once asked a horse for a little food. The horse said, "If anything remains of my midday meal I'll give you something, just because I'm such a generous fellow. If you come to my stall later this evening, I may even give you a little sack of barley." The mule said, "I don't imagine that you'll be quick to give me a greater reward later when you can't be bothered to share your meal now."

A bear from the far north decided to go off and see the world, and it roamed south, visiting many strange kingdoms. One day he came to a pond and saw a flock of birds drinking. Seeing that they raised their heads after every sip, he stopped to ask why.

"We do it to thank the heavens for giving us water," one bird told the bear.

The bear laughed and called them superstitious. A rooster came up to the bear and said, "You are a stranger, and so we forgive your impolite behavior. You may not share our beliefs, but it is rude to say so when you are our guest."

An ant went down to the river to drink. Carried away by the rushing water, it was in danger of drowning. A dove seated on a branch overhead dropped a leaf into the water, and the ant floated away safely. A little later a birdcatcher came along and lay a trap of lime for the dove. The ant, seeing what he was doing, stung the birdcatcher on the foot. In pain, the birdcatcher threw his trap on the ground, and, startled by the noise, the dove flew away.

Once upon a time, when the sun announced that he was going to take a wife, the frogs all croaked loudly, sending a huge clamor into the sky.

Zeus, disturbed by the noise, asked the frogs, "What's the matter?"

The frogs replied, "The sun is single, and even still he dries up our ponds and kills us with his heat. Imagine what would happen if he should father other suns."

A fox, caught in a trap, escaped with only the loss of its brushy tail. Ashamed at his appearance, the fox called his fellow foxes together and advised them to cut off their tails, saying they would look better without them—and besides, they wouldn't have to carry the weight of all that fur.

"Would you be giving us this fashion advice," asked another fox, "if you still had your tail?"

A mouse once nipped at a bull, and the bull, angry, tried to chase the mouse down. The mouse reached its hole safely. The bull dug away at the hole with his horns, and then, exhausted, fell asleep. The mouse scampered out of the hole and bit the bull again. The bull, stamping its hooves, did not know what to do. The mouse said, "See? The strong don't always win."

Once some ants were spending a cold winter day drying out grain that they had collected in summer. A hungry grasshopper happened by and begged for a little food. An ant said, "Why didn't you save any food during the summer?" The grasshopper replied, "I didn't have enough time. I was too busy singing." The ants said, "Well, if you were unwise enough to sing your way through summer, you'll have to dance hungry through winter."

Some frogs once sent a messenger to Zeus and asked him to appoint a king for them. Seeing that they were stupid, Zeus threw a log down into the frogs' pond. The frogs, terrified by the splash, cowered at the bottom of the pond and marveled at the terrible might of their leader. But then they saw that the log did not move, and after a while they came to the surface and squatted on the log. After a while they began to talk, and they agreed that Zeus had sent them an inept ruler.

They sent a second messenger to Zeus asking for another king. Zeus threw an eel into the pond, but the eel hid itself away underwater and refused to be bothered.

The frogs sent a third messenger to Zeus to beg for another, stronger ruler. Now annoyed, Zeus sent them a heron, who preyed on the frogs so voraciously that soon none were left in the pond.

Two men were traveling through the mountains. A bear suddenly came upon them. One of the men climbed up into a tree. The other fell on the ground. The bear came up to the man lying there and sniffed at him. The man pretended to be dead, and the bear left him alone — because, as you know, bears will not bother the dead. But before he departed, the bear whispered something to the man.

The bear shambled off. After a while, the first man climbed down from the tree and asked his friend, "What did the bear say to you?"

"He said," answered the second man, "that I should never travel with anyone who deserts me at the first sign of danger."

A trumpeter marching into battle was captured by the enemy. He cried out, "Please spare my life. I have never slain a single man in combat. I have done nothing to you. I carry no weapons, only this horn."

The enemy commander said, "It's for that very reason that you will now die. For while you yourself do not fight, your trumpet makes others do so."

A caged dove once boasted to a crow about the large number of young that she had hatched. The crow said, "The more children you have, the sorrier you should be, seeing them shut away in this prison."

A skinny wolf once happened to meet a hound, strong and robust. The wolf said hello and praised the hound's good looks. "You could be as sturdy as I am if you wanted," said the hound. "I eat what I want to, whenever I want to. Come with me."

As they were walking along the wolf noticed a flat spot on the hound's neck. "What is that?" the wolf asked.

"Oh, that's just the mark the rope leaves on me after I've been tied up," the hound replied.

"Can't you go wherever you want to?" asked the wolf.

"No," said the hound, "but what does it matter as long as I'm well fed?"

"It matters a lot," said the wolf, running back into the forest.

—THE END—

The Girl Who Made Stars
and Other Bushman Stories

These beautiful and timeless stories from the African Bush were gathered more than a century ago and have touched thousands of readers ever since. Laurens van der Post revered them and helped to make them known throughout the world. For this special new edition, Gregory McNamee has adapted the nineteenth-century original texts to create modern versions meant for readers without prior knowledge of Bushman ways of life.

The stories in this book carry universal observations and truths and, with their historical and ethnographic roots in the African Bushman culture, they are fascinating and educational for readers and listeners of all ages. They bear powerful testimony to a desert people living at one with Nature.

150 pages, ISBN 3-85630-599-8

The Bearskin Quiver
A Collection of Southwestern American Indian Folktales

In this charming collection of folktales from long ago, we read of the creation of the world, of the ways of animals, of the beguiling Coyote, of the world in which we live and other worlds that hide just beyond our sight. Drawn from the oral literatures of some twenty Southwestern American Indian peoples, these stories teach us about the constants of those dry places: about how the clouds form in the sky, how the heat rises from the ground, how the animals move about from one shady spot to another, and how the people once lived their lives. All these stories show us – as the great anthropologist, Claude Lévi-Strauss, observed – that folktales are not mere afterthoughts of literature, just pleasant stories to tell around the campfire, but rather valuable tools for reflection upon our own lives.

139 pages, ISBN 3-85630-610-2

The Rock Rabbit and The Rainbow
Laurens van der Post among Friends

Sir Laurens van der Post, author, film-maker, storyteller of worldwide renown, soldier, prisoner of war, political advisor to heads of state, humanitarian, explorer, conservationist ... the list goes on and on. His extraordinary curiosity, his love for the small and the great, and his tremendous feeling and concern for his surroundings and all that they included, set him traveling the lands and the waters of the world, a messenger in search of meaning. He touched and inspired many along the way, some of whom are to be found in the pages of this book.

The Rock Rabbit
and
The Rainbow

Laurens van der Post
among Friends

A true man of his time, Sir Laurens was born in 1906 in the interior of South Africa, served in the British forces during World War II, including three-and-a-half years in Japanese captivity, and lived and worked since that time in London, where he died just after celebrating his 90th birthday in December, 1996.

The Rock Rabbit and The Rainbow was originally conceived as a Festschrift, or gift collection of writings, for Sir Laurens by several of his friends and then evolved into its present form, which includes numerous original contributions by Sir Laurens himself.

hardcover, 400 pages, illustrated, ISBN 3-85630-512-2

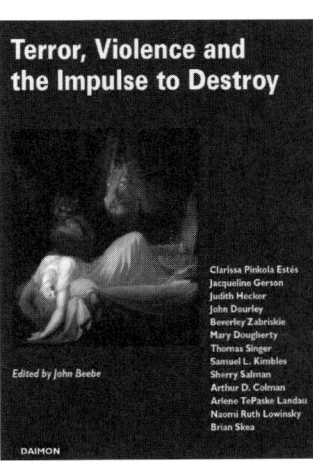

Terror, Violence and the Impulse to Destroy
John Beebe (Ed.)

These papers from the North American Conference of Jungian Analysts address the process of terror as it confronts us in international situations and in outbreaks of violence in homes and schools. The thirteen contributors, seasoned Jungian analysts and psychotherapists, have often faced the reality of undermining destructiveness in their work with clients. Here they offer their theoretical and therapeutic insights, drawing from their experience of the psyche's healing resources to identify the consciousness we need if we are to survive and reverse the contagion of hostility. 410 pages, illustrated, ISBN 3-85630-628-5

English Titles from Daimon

English Titles from Daimon

Laurens van der Post - *The Rock Rabbit and the Rainbow*
Jane Reid - *Jung, My Mother and I: The Analytic Diaries*
of Catharine Rush Cabot
R.M. Rilke - *Duino Elegies*
Miguel Serrano - *C.G. Jung and Hermann Hesse*
Helene Shulman - *Living at the Edge of Chaos*
Dennis Slattery / Lionel Corbet (Eds.)
- *Depth Psychology: Meditations on the Field*
Susan Tiberghien - *Looking for Gold*
Ann Ulanov - *Spiritual Aspects of Clinical Work*
- *Picturing God*
- *Receiving Woman*
- *The Female Ancestors of Christ*
- *The Wisdom of the Psyche*
- *The Wizards' Gate, Picturing Consciousness*
Ann & Barry Ulanov - *Cinderella and her Sisters: The Envied*
and the Envying
- *Healing Imagination: Psyche and Soul*
Erlo van Waveren - *Pilgrimage to the Rebirth*
Harry Wilmer - *How Dreams Help*
- *Quest for Silence*
Luigi Zoja - *Drugs, Addiction and Initiation*
Luigi Zoja & Donald Williams - *Jungian Reflections on September 11*
Jungian Congress Papers - *Jerusalem 1983: Symbolic & Clinical Approaches*
- *Berlin 1986: Archetype of Shadow in a Split World*
- *Paris 1989: Dynamics in Relationship*
- *Chicago 1992: The Transcendent Function*
- *Zürich 1995: Open Questions*
- *Florence 1998: Destruction and Creation*
- *Cambridge 2001*

Available from your bookstore or from our distributors:

In the United States:

Bookworld Trade Inc.
1941 Whitfield Park Loop
Sarasota FL 34243
Please order on the web: www.bookworld.com
Fax: 800-777-2525 Phone: 800-444-2524

In Great Britain:

Airlift Book Company
8 The Arena
Enfield, Middlesex EN3 7NJ
Phone: (0181) 804 0400
Fax: (0181) 804 0044

Worldwide:

Daimon Verlag   Hauptstrasse 85   CH-8840 Einsiedeln   Switzerland
Phone: (41)(55) 412 2266   Fax: (41)(55) 412 2231
email: info@daimon.ch

*Visit our website: **www.daimon.ch***
or write for our complete catalog